First edition August 2015.

ISBN: 978-0-9860590-3-2   (Trade Paper)
ISBN: 978-0-9860590-4-9   (eBook: EPUB)
ISBN: 978-0-9860590-5-6   (eBook: MOBI)

Library of Congress Cataloging-in-Publication Data
Gale, Geri. *Alex: The Double-Rescue Dog* / by Geri Gale; illustrated by Pamela Farrington. 1st edition p. cm.
Summary: A true story of how a dog named Alex was double-rescued by two moms.
ISBN-13: 978-0-9860590-3-2 (trade) / ISBN-10: 0-986-05903-X (trade)
1. Children's—Fiction. 2. LGBT—Fiction. 3. Dogs—Fiction.
4. Jewish—Fiction. 5. Japanese-American—Fiction. I. Title.
Library of Congress Control Number: 2015941054

Printed in the United States of America.

PK & Alex Co.
4616 25th Avenue NE #363
Seattle, WA 98105
gerigale.com

Special thanks to editor/coach TJ Hatfield; copyeditors/proofreaders
Michael Mendonsa and Amy Davis for their careful reviews of the manuscript.

The illustrations were rendered with ink and watercolor.
The text was set in Rockwell. Book design by Pamela Farrington.

To my beloved dogs Sasha, Noma, Rose, Hobo, Althea, Sammy, and Alex

For the other dogs in my life: Rufus, D.O.G., Tora, Honda, Cody, Emerson,
Rocky, Midge, Pepper, Chewy, Lucy, Raymond, Junior, Miteka, Bella,
Izzy, Tanner, Carmen, Gabby, Nikki, Chloe, Auggie, Regan, Zepar, Brenna,
Sinister, Sylph, Buster, Olive, Tobi, Bette, Vida, Herschel, and Blu

For sisters Patty and Janice Kunitsugu

Alex: The Double-Rescue Dog

By Geri Gale

Illustrated by Pamela Farrington

Geri Gale
august 2015

My name is
Alex

This is a true story.

My first people LOOOOOOVED me.

My mother loved to lick my left ear.
She would whisper,
"You're so cute.
I could eat you up."

She didn't care that
I had a pink eye
and a bowed leg.

One Sunday morning,
I barked a harrowing goodbye
to my two sisters and mother.
Even the cows, horses, sheep,
and chickens had never heard
such a terrible cry.
I was driven off.
I watched our barn fade away.
I didn't understand
why I had to leave.

The California sun shined all the time and I ran by myself

like a wild and crazy dog chasing birds in my new fenced yard.

In the mornings, I was dressed up for a play.

I was a Harley biker, a pirate, a chef.

I sat on the little girl's lap while

she read happy stories to me.

When she got home from school,

she set the table for

tea parties, and she

made me wear

a bow tie.

And then her dad lost his job. Every day he went looking for a new one.

Every day he came home, sad in the eyes, without a smile, and with a

ghostlike face. One day a sign popped up in the yard.

Then came my second
car ride and the words,
"Sorry little guy. We can't
afford to buy you any more
food. It's time for you to find
a new home."

He opened the door. I was
afraid to jump out. I looked
him in the eyes, but he
would not look at me.
"You'll have a better life
someplace else,"
he said, rubbing
behind my ears.

His eyes filled with tears,
and he lifted me off his lap

and
gently
put me
on the
ground.
I watched
him drive
a w a y.

NO DOGS
ON ROAD

There was no one to tell me what to do.
I didn't have to dress up in funny clothes,
and I was free to explore on my own. But
it wasn't the same. This time I was *really*
alone. The neighborhood smelled—yucky
garbage, old fried food, stinky fish, rotten
eggs, exhaust fumes, and dirty diapers.
I was scared. I almost got hit by a car.

The nights were DARK.

I missed my mother and sisters.

I hid and slept by the river in a wobbly cardboard box.

I kept quiet and still,
pretending I was invisible
so all the wild-in-the-night
creatures roaming the
riverbank wouldn't find me.

I lived
on
crumbs
and
berries.

One day I ate a worm.

On the seventh day it rained and thunder struck.

My cardboard box floated down the river.

At the end of the river, a man with jangling keys gave me a piece of chicken jerky. It was yummy, but it came with a net. He scooped me up and locked me in a cage in a van filled with 30 other dogs. We were all scared. Even the tough dudes.

A German shepherd said, "Something's really wrong out there. They're dumping us on the streets like cats."

A Siberian husky said, "They can't feed us anymore."

A golden retriever said, "They're losing their jobs."

A poodle asked, "Where do you think they're taking us?"

A Jack Russell said, "No one's telling us a thing."

We rode

and rode for

two days and

two nights.

A thousand

miles later,

we pulled

into a

parking lot

at a Chinese

restaurant in

Washington.

Outside the sun peeked through gray clouds shaped like a golden castle.

Everything was moving fast. People were
frantically picking out dogs and snatching
them up. The loud coos and excited squeals
hurt my ears. No one even looked at me.

I still had the pink eye and the
bowed leg, and now that I'd been
hungry for so long, I was scrappy,
thin, and sickly looking too.

One by one, dogs disappeared.
I stood alone. No one wanted me.
All those people out there—
and not one of them wanted me.
I started to cry. I couldn't help it.

I hid my eyes under my paws.

Click. Click. Click. A burst of light
and a woman with black hair, wearing
a black glittered shirt, jeans, sandals,
and hearts on her socks appeared.
Her camera flashed like a magic wand.

She yelled to her friend,
"Geri, come see this little guy."

Geri turned her back on us and said,
"PK wants a poodle."

The woman with the camera picked
me up and said, "I'm going to show
you to my sister PK. **She'll love you**."

PK, the woman with the funny name, appeared.

Geri followed PK. We all trailed behind PK,

and every time PK petted someone,

the woman with the camera would say,

"That dog looks like a biter."

"I bet that one doesn't like to cuddle."

"I'm sure that one barks all the time."

When PK took a break in her search,
the woman with the camera put me
in Geri's arms. I nestled against her chest.
Geri looked straight into my eyes.
She rubbed my pink eye and
touched my bowed leg.
I licked her face. She hugged me
and gave me a kiss on my left ear.

PK saw me in Geri's arms.
She melted.

"He's the one," PK said.

Next thing I knew, I was sitting on Geri's lap in the backseat of a big silver car.

The two sisters sat in the front. (They reminded me of my sisters. Always telling each other what to do!) During that first car ride in Seattle, while PK drove up hills and over bridges, one hundred pictures were taken of me in Geri's arms.

When I looked through the window and saw the majestic,

snowcapped mountain in the cloudless blue sky, I felt as

if the camera was sprinkling magic dust ✳ ✳ ✳ ✳ ✳ ✳ ✳

all
around
us.

Geri stroked my matted fur.
But still, I wondered, "Did she
and PK really want me?"
She told me she was Jewish
and this was a mitzvah and
she needed me in her life
as much as I needed her.
A few blocks later, she said,
"Alexander."

PK hemmed, "I can't
call a dog, 'Alexander'."
"Alex," said Geri.
"Alex," PK agreed.

The car came to a stop. I was
nervous. I climbed out onto
a small patch of grass. In the
house I sniffed every room—
the kitchen floor, the living
room couch, the carpet,
upstairs, downstairs. It wasn't
too big. Not a lot to guard.
And it wasn't too small.
There were plenty of spaces
to hide. I found a cave in the
corner and I established a
lookout by the front window.

That's when I saw them.

B I R D S !

Tons of birds,
different from the ones
in California, but still
perfect for chasing.

Geri and PK watched me watching the birds,
my tail wagging like a windshield wiper.
I saw them hug each other. The tears in
their eyes were happy tears. I know because
I swallowed happy tears too. That's when I
figured it out. This was my forever home,
and I was double-rescued—by my two moms.

Now that I lived in the city, I had to wear a glow-in-the-
dark harness and a winter raincoat! But that was okay,
because it didn't take long to realize that Geri and PK
weren't going to send me back to California.

Instead they took me to doggie school, where
I learned how to do Commando Crawl, how to wait,
fetch, high-five, and twirl like a circus dog.

Everything was perfect.

Then my Mom Geri learned she had breast cancer.

The next night the three of us snuggled together on the couch.

Geri and PK both seemed sad and happy at the same time.

I gave them lots of doggie licks and pranced around

like a tough guy showing off my bowed leg.

They laughed so hard, their dark sadness left the room.

PK said, "I'll always protect both of you. Together we can do this."

Geri said, "All along I thought we rescued you,

but really you're the one who rescued me."

the end.

AUTHOR'S NOTE

This story is based on a true story. I wrote it during my weekly chemo treatments from February to August 2013.

Alex met Lucy in the neighborhood. She was the most beautiful dog he'd ever seen. On September 26, 2010, they got married at Fido Fest in the Chapel of Dog Love. He even wore a bow tie again!

On December 6, 2012, Geri and PK were issued marriage license #357 in Seattle. On December 9, 2012, Geri and PK were married at City Hall in Seattle. They had met in 1978 and had been together for 35 years.

Some of the proceeds of this book will be donated to PAWS and the Swedish Cancer Institute.

PAWS is an organization in Lynnwood, Washington, which is a champion for animals—rehabilitating injured and orphaned wildlife, sheltering and adopting homeless dogs and cats, and educating people to make a better world for animals and people.

Swedish Cancer Institute is a Seattle-area leader in diagnosis, treatment, and recovery of cancer. Teams include a host of oncologists—doctors focused exclusively on the care and treatment of cancer, using medication, radiation, and other therapies. They work in a collaborative, multidisciplinary environment that focuses on the patient—not the disease.

ACKNOWLEDGMENTS

For Janice Kunitsugu, the woman with the camera who found and chose Alex at a Chinese restaurant parking lot in Seattle. A special thanks to TJ Hatfield. She read my manuscript and tightened and shaped it as a writer and mother who understands the voice of a children's book. Without her, without this collaboration, this book would not be in its current form. It would have been the length of a very long novel. And it would lack her sense of a *glass-is-full world.* She added sweeping brushstrokes of happy-word polish to every single page.

I love collaborating with artist Pamela Farrington. She always finds the visual thread of my stories, and her illustrations and design add brilliance to this simple story about a much-loved rescue dog.

For Michael Mendonsa and Amy Davis; they carefully read each word to make perfection on each page. Lori Mahoney added the final touches—she is a gem.

For the Third Sunday writers—Priscilla Long, Jack Remick, M. Anne Sweet, Gordon H. Wood, Don Harmon, and Matt Rizzo—who helped strengthen my sentences.

For Patricia E. Gale, Jaclynn Hiranaka, Scott Parducci, Leah Elgin, Amy Doerzbacher, Dee Paiement, Sue Mings, Phileo McAlexander, Melissa Bertocchini, Sandy Poliachik, Jessica Sari Rosenberg, Lynda Sisley, Gary Gale, Kymberly Gale, Andrew Gale, Greg Gale, Melodie Schneider, Racelle Bustrup, Mallory Olson, Dr. Claire Buchanan, Dr. Kristine Rinn, Dr. Vivek Mehta, Meaghan Hession-Herzog, Linda Willsie, Catie Barkston, Makenna Reeves, Andrea Stone, Linda McVay, Lois Sax, Ginger Luke, Dina Okimoto, Elena Meeker, UCLA, Strut the Pup, and the Maple Leaf Vet—the friends of Alex.

About the Author and Illustrator

Geri Gale is a poet and a writer of prose. Her books include *Patrice: a poemella* and *Waiting* (from *The Gerund Collection*). Her poetry and prose have appeared in numerous publications. For more details about past and future works, visit gerigale.com.

Pamela Farrington is a graphic designer and illustrator. She also creates shrines that become altars for dreams, aspirations, good health, love, and the future. Her design company is Velvet Design Studio. Visit velvetdesignstudio.com.

Made in the USA
San Bernardino, CA
16 August 2015